We are
FAMILY

Whoever we are and whatever we do,
Our families hold us together like glue.

Whenever we need them, they'll come when we call,
They're ready to catch us, if ever we fall.

For Rob, Lucy and Rosie – *my* happy family
~ PH

For my family, whose support has been immeasurable
~ RW

CATERPILLAR BOOKS
An imprint of the Little Tiger Group
www.littletiger.co.uk
1 The Coda Centre, 189 Munster Road, London SW6 6AW
This edition published in Great Britain 2017

ISBN: 978-1-84857-643-8
CPB/1400/0700/0417
2 4 6 8 10 9 7 5 3 1

We are FAMILY

Patricia Hegarty
Illustrated by Ryan Wheatcroft

Wherever we are, whatever the weather,
Families always stick together.

Through thick and through thin, happy and sad,
We're there for each other, in good times and bad.

Mornings are busy – we hurry about,
Rushing backwards and forwards, before we go out.

We may eat at the table, on our laps or a tray,
Spending time together, before starting our day.

When it's time for school, we bolt out the door,
Keen to find out what the day has in store.

Our journeys are different, by bus, bike or car,
But families are with us, wherever we are.

When we feel poorly, and stay in our beds,
Families are there to soothe aching heads.

They'll comfort and nurse us and take special care,
And we'll be so thankful our loved ones are there.

Sometimes we go on holidays or happy fun days out.
Doing things together is what families are about.

The beach, the park, the countryside, any special place –
We'll kick a ball, fly a kite or play a game of chase.

If something awful happens, it happens to us all:
A fire, a flood, an illness, disappointment or a fall.

We'll cope with it together, a family, as one,
Until the clouds have lifted and we can see the Sun.

Families are loving, they're strong and kind and caring.
We're there for one another; a problem is for sharing.

We work at things together, we feel each other's pain.
We're the silver lining, the sunshine after rain.

When the day is over, tucked up in our beds,
All sorts of thoughts and dreams fill our sleepy heads.

After goodnight kisses, with our families all round,
We drift off to dreamland, loved and safe and sound.

Each family is different, it may be large or small.
We may look like each other – or not alike at all.

Money doesn't matter, nor colour, creed, nor name –
In each and every family, the love we feel's the same.